Math in the Bath

(and other fun places, too!)

by Sara Atherlay

illustrated by Megan Halsey

Simon & Schuster Books for Young Readers

SIMON & SCHUSTER BOOKS FOR YOUNG READERS
An imprint of Simon & Schuster Children's Publishing Division
1230 Avenue of the Americas, New York, New York 10020

Book design by Cathy Bobak
The text of this book is set in 18 point Helvetica.
The illustrations are rendered in gouache, gesso, pastel, and colored pencil
on hot-pressed watercolor paper.
Printed in Hong Kong by South China Printing Company (1988) Ltd.
First edition
10 9 8 7 6 5 4 3

Library of Congress Cataloging-in-Publication Data
Atherlay, Sara.
    Math in the Bath / and other fun places, too / by Sara Atherlay ;
illustrated by Megan Halsey. — 1st ed.
        p. cm.
    ISBN 0-689-80318-4
        1. Mathematics—Study and teaching (Elementary). I. Halsey, Megan. II. Title.
QA135.5.A835   1995
649' .68—dc20   94-30264

To parents and teachers:

Have you ever decided that a certain box would never fit through a door, without bothering to measure it, or planned how many chairs you'd have to borrow for a dinner party? If you have, then you've been estimating and problem solving. Without even thinking about it, you've been using math. Math is all around us, and we use it and see it everywhere and every day.

This book wasn't written to teach a particular math concept, but to make math less abstract and give it relevance. It started as a way to encourage my class to examine their day to find where math lies. In the process, they not only discovered that math is everywhere but how math works. Eventually, the book began to grow as my young students wrote their own versions, broadening each section and even adding new ones. As their understanding developed, more sophisticated examples of math were found. These discoveries made the more formal learning of math easier to master, because it had become meaningful.

Use this book as a launch to a math-friendly world. Our number and math systems are based on patterns, so help your children to discover math in clothes and fabrics by recognizing repeating shapes (pattern recognition). Encourage them to estimate the number of people who will arrive at a party so they can predict how many cookies to bake. Listen to all kinds of music, and count rhythms and beats. You will be helping them to see that finding math is useful, that math makes sense, and that math is fun!

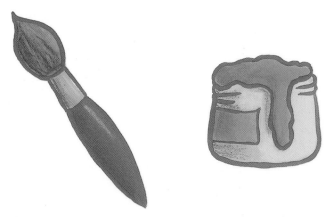

Where is math in the morning?

7:00 A.M.! Time to wake up.
One pair of socks,

one pair of shoes,

for one pair of feet.

Count by twos the steps to school.
See you at 3:00 P.M.

Where is math in the classroom?

One desk for every chair.
How many sets all together?

Six boys, six girls. . . .

A dozen friends
finding math everywhere!

Math detectives!

Where is math in music?

3/4, 4/4, 6/8 time.
Snapping, clapping,
tapping rhythms.

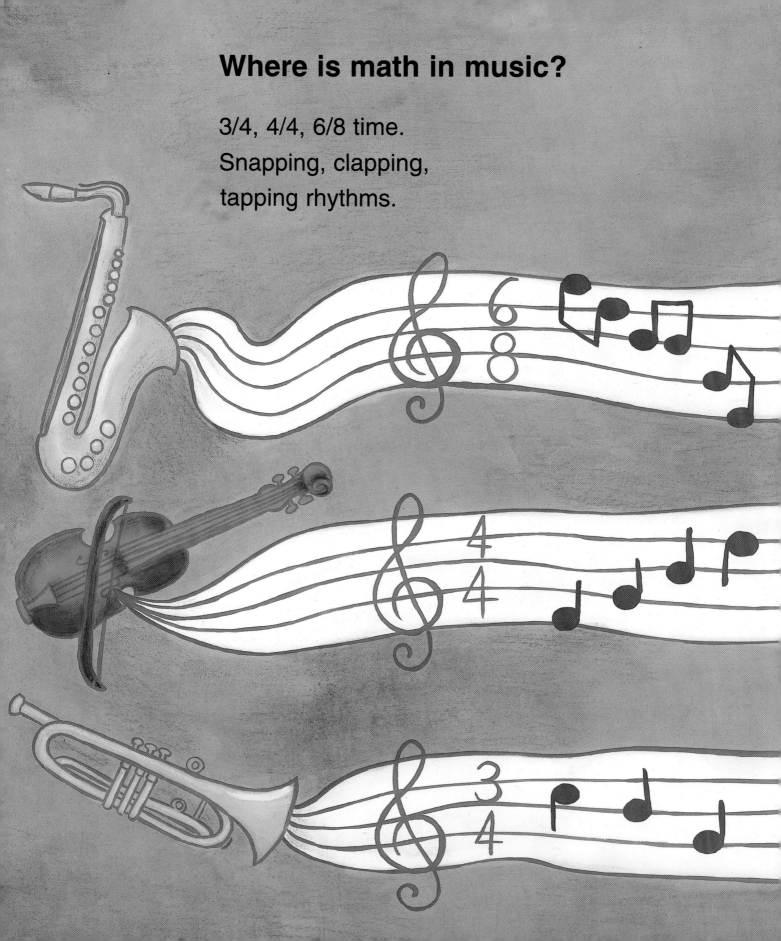

Count it steady.
Fast and slow.
Big bright music!

Where is math in art?

Circles, triangles, squares.
Sailing on a sunny day,
shapes are all around.

A little more yellow + a little less blue = rich, green grass:
Math magic created by you.

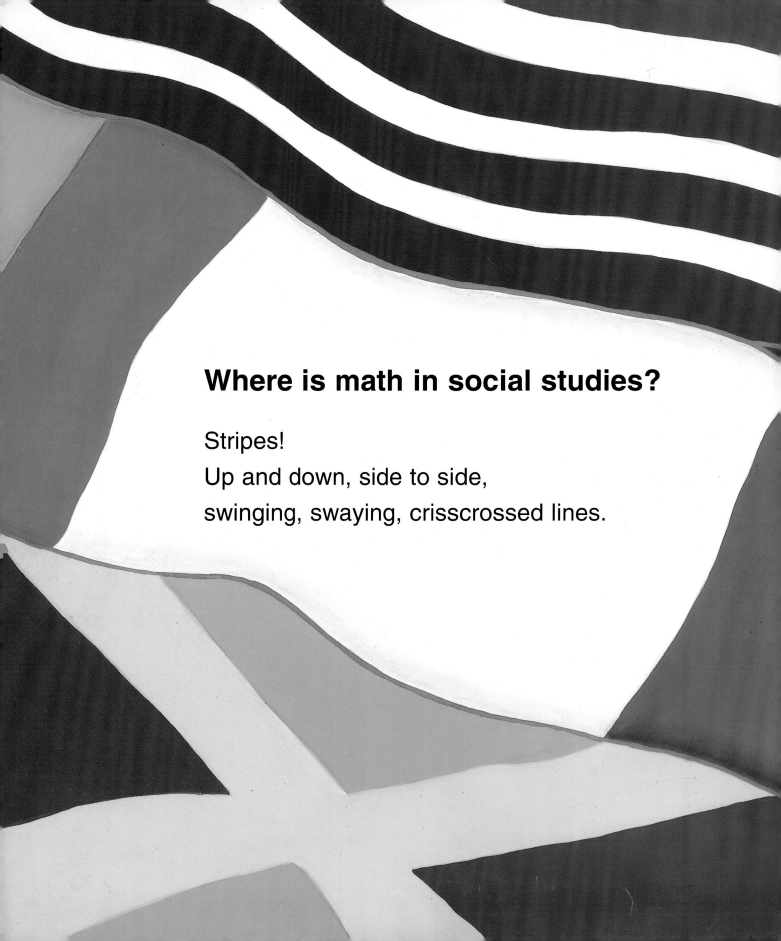

Where is math in social studies?

Stripes!
Up and down, side to side,
swinging, swaying, crisscrossed lines.

Patterns of pride!

Where is math in recess?

Kick the ball: Far, farther, farthest.
Round first base, second base, third . . .

Slide home: Close, closer, closest.

Score!
Have fun!

Where is math in nature?

Long bugs, short bugs, wide bugs, narrow bugs.
Deep-in-the-ground bugs.
High-in-the-tree bugs.

Eight legs: spiders.
Six legs: beetles, ants, and butterflies.
Creepy, crawly dimensions.

Where is math in dinnertime?

One whole pizza pie:

Two toppings to choose.

Three slices with peppers: 3/8.

Four slices with pepperoni: 1/2.

(How many slices are plain?)

Five hungry stomachs.

Yum!

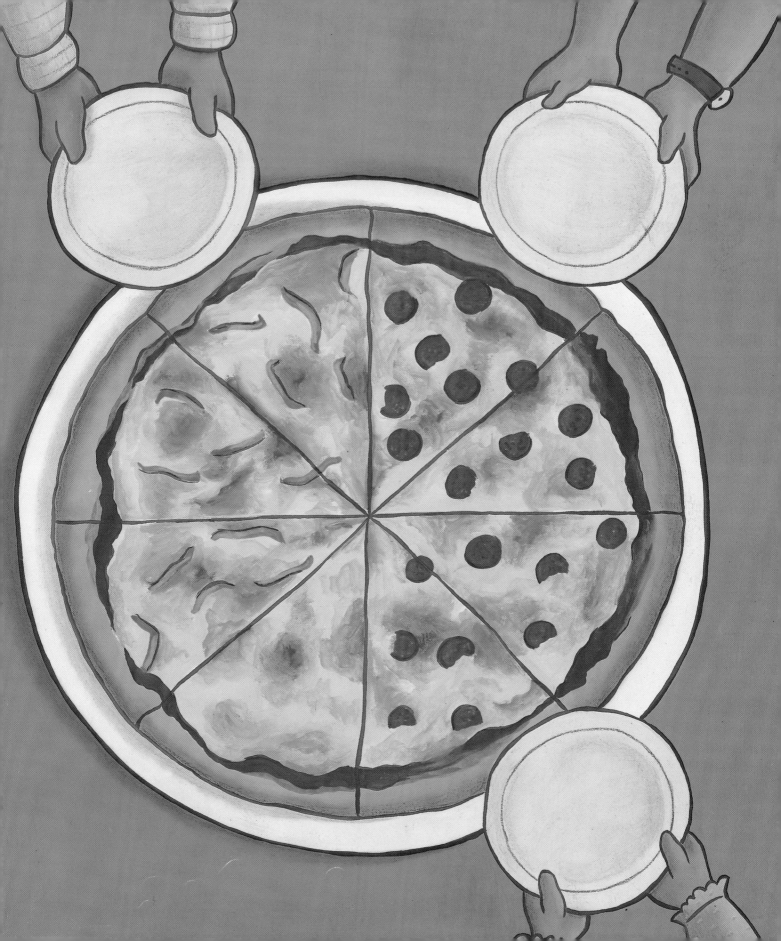

Where is math in family?

If Grandma, Zoe, and Stephen
go to the beach in a van,
then how many of us are left
to ride in the car?

Problem solved.

Where is math at bath time?

7:00 P.M.
Bath math!
The more soap in the water,
the more bubbles we'll have!

Where is math at bedtime?

Two stories for you, two stories for me.
Five more minutes, please?
One sheep,
two sheep,
three sheep, four . . .

Good night.

Math is everywhere! Look for it!

Attributes: Thick, thin, short or tall, everything has width, depth, and height, and comes in different sizes. Look and compare.

Counting: Count marbles, stones, or footsteps. Two at a time is the speedy way to count! Two, four, six, eight, ten, twelve . . .

Estimating: Look at a ruler, then hide it behind you. Now, guess how many rulers, or feet, it would take to reach the wall, the end of the hallway, or the edge of the playground.

Fractions: Equal shares mean fair shares. Use fractions to divide cookies, and share them with your friends.

Grouping: A set of four books, a set of eight markers. What other sets do you have around the house?

More and less: Add more bubble bath to the water, and you make it more bubbly. Take away carrot sticks from your plate, and you have less. What else can you add? What else can you subtract?

Patterns: Numbers and math are always in patterns. Flags have stripes, music has rhythms. What other patterns can you find?

Shapes: Look at your bed. Look at your plate. You can find shapes all around you.

Sorting: Mismatched shoes and socks would be so silly! Match them up so they make sense.

Tell time: How many minutes until playtime? How many hours until dinner? Telling time helps you know when things happen.